BUSTER
catches a cold

By Hisako Madokoro   English text by Patricia Lantier   Illustrated by Ken Kuroi

For a free color catalog describing Gareth Stevens' list of high-quality children's books, call 1-800-341-3569 (USA) or 1-800-461-9120 (Canada).

Library of Congress Cataloging-in-Publication Data

Madokoro, Hisako, 1938-
  [Ame no hi no Korowan. English]
  Buster catches a cold / text by Hisako Madokoro ;
illustrations by Ken Kuroi.
    p.   cm. — (The Adventures of Buster the puppy)
  Translation of: Ame no hi no Korowan.
  Summary: Buster the puppy ignores his mother's
instructions and goes outside for an adventure in
the rain.
  ISBN 0-8368-0489-9
  [1. Dogs—Fiction. 2. Rain and rainfall—Fiction.]
I. Kuroi, Ken, 1947- ill. II. Title. III. Series:
Madokoro, Hisako, 1938- Korowan. English.
PZ7.M2657Bub 1991
[E]—dc20   90-47948

North American edition first published in 1991 by
Gareth Stevens Children's Books
1555 North RiverCenter Drive, Suite 201
Milwaukee, Wisconsin 53212, USA

This U.S. edition copyright © 1991. Text
copyright © 1991 by Gareth Stevens, Inc. First
published as *Ame No Hi No Korowan* (*Korowan in
the Rain*) in Japan with an original copyright
© 1983 by Hisako Madokoro (text) and Ken Kuroi
(illustrations). English translation rights arranged
with CHILD HONSHA through Japan Foreign-
Rights Centre.

Cover design: Kristi Ludwig

Printed in the United States of America

1 2 3 4 5 6 7 8 9 97 96 95 94 93 92 91

Gareth Stevens Children's Books
MILWAUKEE

2

"Don't go out in the rain, Buster," said his mother. "You'll catch a nasty cold."

4

Buster waited until his mother was asleep. Then he tiptoed outside. "I wonder what a cold is," he thought to himself.

5

"If I see something that looks
like it might be a cold, I'll
be sure not to catch it,"
he decided.

7

A frog jumped out of
a flowering bush.
"Yipes!" cried Buster.
"A cold!"

"I'm not a cold," said the
frog. "I'm a frog."

"C'mon, let's play tag!"

11

Buster saw a snail on a leaf.
He stood on a stone for a
closer look. "Are you a
cold?" he asked the snail.

13

"Of course I'm not a cold,"
said the snail as he crawled
away through a puddle.

14

16

The frog hopped away, too,
and Buster was left alone
in the rain.

"I don't think I'll ever see
a cold!" he thought,
and shivered.

18

Suddenly, Buster saw a
huge puddle in front of him.
"I wonder if colds live in
puddles," he thought.

Buster stared into the water.
Staring back at him was a
terrible face with a big
pink tongue.

"Help!" Buster cried.
"A cold!"

Buster hit the face with his paw and got even wetter himself. "Ah-choo!" sneezed Buster, and he ran for home.

Ah-choo! "AH-CHOOOO!"

"I said you'd catch a cold,"
said his mother, covering him
with a warm blanket.

"Sorry, Mother," said Buster.
"But I did enjoy the rain.
Ah-choo!"